Belmont and the Dragon

Danger in Redwitch Village

CANCELLED Mike Zarb

Robin Gold

RANDOM HOUSE AUSTRALIA

Addresses for companies within the Random House Group can be
found at www.randomhouse.com.au/offices.

National Library of Australia
Cataloguing-in-Publication Entry

Author: Gold, Robin
Title: Danger in Redwitch Village / Robin Gold, illustrated by Mike Zarb
ISBN: 978 1 86471 969 7 (pbk.)
Series: Gold, Robin. Belmont and the dragon; 4
Target Audience: For primary school age
Other Authors/Contributors: Zarb, Michael
Dewey Number: A823.4

Cover illustration by Mike Zarb
Cover and text layout by Jobi Murphy
Printed and bound by 1010 International
Printing Limited
10 9 8 7 6 5 4 3 2 1

For our servicemen and women,
brave knights all – MZ

For Mrs Brown,
who encouraged me to write – RG

Long, long ago in the madcap medieval metropolis of Old York there lived two best friends: a boy called Belmont and a dragon called Burnie.

A Royal Edict

His Most Excellent Majesty
King Cyrus
and
Her Royal Highness
Princess Libby

will present a gift to the good
citizens of the kingdom of
Old York.

Special unveiling
on
Old York Day

Every year on Old York Day the citizens celebrated with ticker-tape parades, marching bands, flags and fireworks!

King Cyrus and Princess Libby issued a royal decree promising their subjects a very special gift to honour the occasion. The exact nature of the gift was a closely guarded secret and pretty soon the entire kingdom was abuzz with speculation.

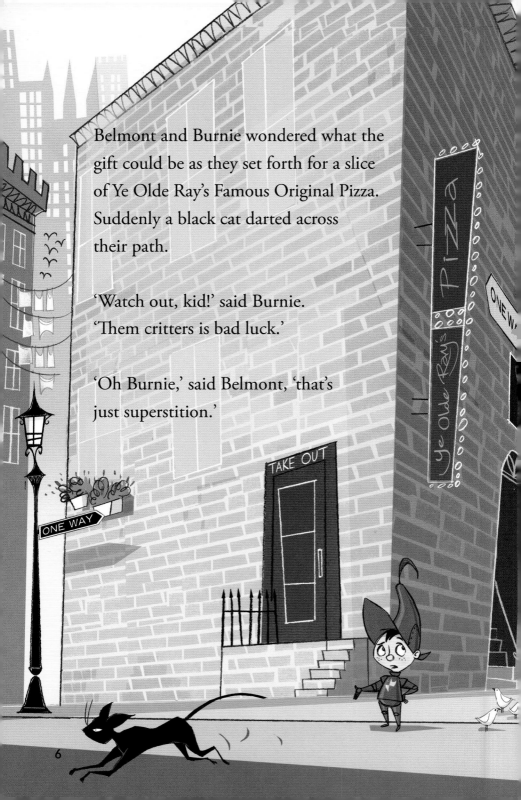

Belmont and Burnie wondered what the gift could be as they set forth for a slice of Ye Olde Ray's Famous Original Pizza. Suddenly a black cat darted across their path.

'Watch out, kid!' said Burnie. 'Them critters is bad luck.'

'Oh Burnie,' said Belmont, 'that's just superstition.'

'Well, they're bad luck for me,' said Burnie. 'I'm allergic!'

At that moment three
Beastly Bedraggled Batniks
scurried towards them at
breakneck speed.

They hauled a red wagon carrying something large and heavy.

'Look out, kid!' yelped Burnie. But it was too late …

SPLAM! Everybody went flying!

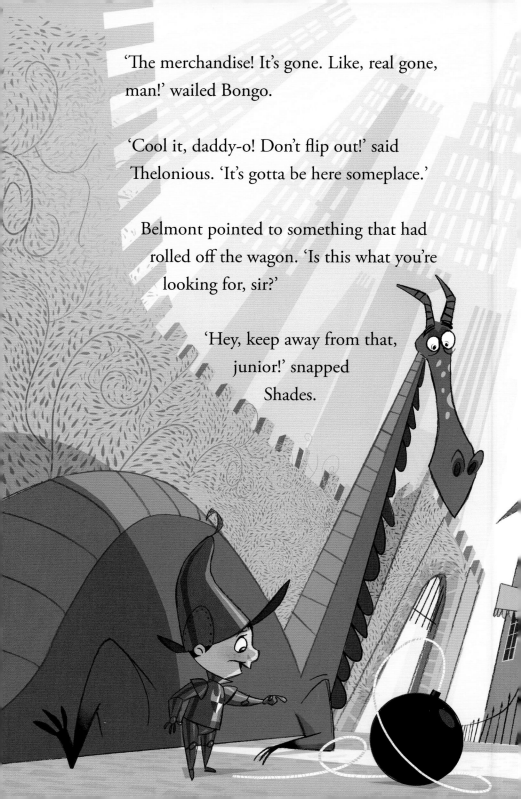

'The merchandise! It's gone. Like, real gone, man!' wailed Bongo.

'Cool it, daddy-o! Don't flip out!' said Thelonious. 'It's gotta be here someplace.'

Belmont pointed to something that had rolled off the wagon. 'Is this what you're looking for, sir?'

'Hey, keep away from that, junior!' snapped Shades.

Bongo and Thelonious hoisted the object
carefully onto the wagon.

'I'm sorry if we got in your
way …' began Belmont.

'No time to shoot the
breeze, man,' said
Thelonious. 'We've gotta
split.'

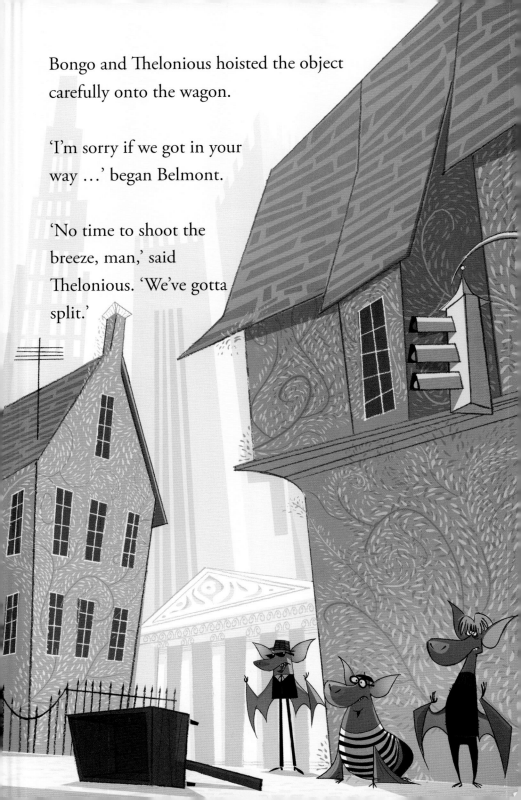

The batniks ran off into the night with their wagon in tow.

'Did you catch what language they were speakin'?' said Burnie, scratching his head.

'I say! You there!' called a voice in the night. A familiar figure hurried towards them.

'Which way did they go?' wheezed Professor I.Q. Cranium, the well-known scientific genius.

'Something wrong, Professor?' asked Belmont.

'Those scoundrels have stolen the Kablooey!'

'The Kablooey?' cried Burnie. 'Not the Kablooey! *Anything* but the Kablooey! One small question … what's a Kablooey?'

'It was during some Top Secret experiments at the Shvitzonian Institute,' explained Professor Cranium, 'I stumbled upon a mysterious compound that can blow solid matter into itsy-bitsy, teensy-weensy pieces.

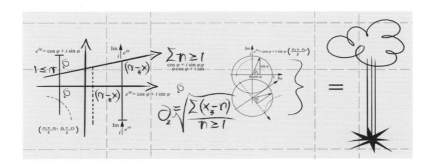

'I called my discovery *Kablooey*.'

'I kept it safely under lock and key,' he continued,
'until those ruffians burst in and forced me to hand it
over. Old York is in the most terrible danger!'

'We'll get your Kablooey back again, Professor, never you fear!' declared Belmont. 'C'mon, Burnie. They went that-a-way.'

They pursued the batniks deep into strange and unfamiliar neighbourhoods, staying well out of sight. Finally they arrived on the bleakest street in Redwitch Village.

Belmont and Burnie hid in the shadows as the batniks
entered a swingin' hangout known as The Cave.

'Now's our chance,' said Belmont. 'If only we had some kind of disguise, so we could blend in with the crowd.'

'I know the very thing, kid,' said Burnie. 'Follow me!'

'We've got the merchandise, Boss,' said Bongo, 'just like you told us.'

'Nice work, boys,' replied The Boss. 'Park it over there in the corner. Now, shouldn't you be up on stage entertaining the customers?'

THE BOSS

TONIGHT!
THE
MAYNARD G.
KREEPS

TICKETS

Moments later, Belmont and Burnie entered The Cave,
cleverly disguised as swinging hepcats.

They saw the batniks emerging empty-handed from
the back room.

STRICTLY
NO
SQUARES

The batniks mounted the stage and began to play …

... as Belmont and Burnie crept
quietly to the back room door.

'S-somethin' itchin' up m' nose,' whispered Burnie. 'Must be a cat 'round here someplace.'

Belmont tried the door handle.

'Locked and bolted,' he said. 'Wait! I can hear voices.'

'What are they sayin', kid?'

Belmont and Burnie each put an ear to the door.

'Okay, Silas,' said the voice from within. 'This is the plan, so listen carefully. When Old York Day comes around we'll hide the Kablooey inside the king's palace. Right in the middle of the celebrations – *Kablooey!* – we'll blow the palace to bits. There'll be so much confusion I can walk right in and take over the joint. Then Old York will be mine ... *all mine!*'

Unable to bear Burnie's weight any longer, the rusted old hinges suddenly popped and the door plunged inwards with a terrific **KRASH!** The two friends were hurled into the back room but Belmont leapt to his feet in a flash.

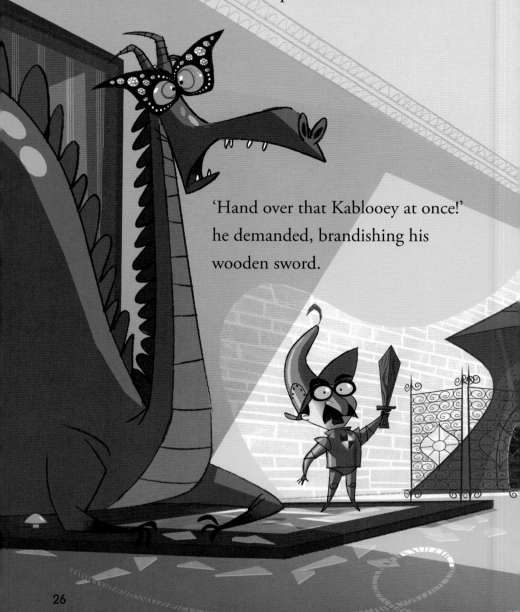

'Hand over that Kablooey at once!' he demanded, brandishing his wooden sword.

'How dare you come busting in here like this?' said The Boss angrily.

'Jumpin' Jabberwockies!' exclaimed Burnie. 'It's the Redwitch!'

27

'That's my name, don't wear it out.'

Unseen by Belmont or Burnie, she pressed a secret button under her desk.

A light flashed outside. The batniks stopped playing and made a dash for the back room.

'Get 'em, boys,' commanded the Redwitch as the batniks charged in.

Shades swung his saxophone, but Belmont ducked and the instrument struck Thelonious smack in the kisser.

'GERONIMO!' cried Belmont, diving at the batniks.

He fought bravely, but was hopelessly outnumbered.

Soon the batniks had securely bound Belmont and Burnie to a couple of chairs.

'There's something familiar about you two,' said the Redwitch. 'Do I know you, Tall-Dark-and-Gruesome?'

'W-who m-m-me?' Burnie replied.

'What about you, Shorty?' said the witch to Belmont. 'Haven't we met before?'

The Redwitch snatched off their disguises.

'Aha! I knew it!' she shrieked. 'It's that annoying little runt and his big dope of a sidekick!'

A black cat arched its back and hissed at
Belmont and Burnie.

'Shoo, cat,' snuffled Burnie as his
eyes watered and his nose itched.

'Run along … scat … beat it.
C-c-cats make me sn-sn-sn –'

All eyes stared in horror at the Kablooey. Burnie's fiery sneeze had ignited the fuse! The burning wick sizzled and spat!

'When that thing blows its top,' said Bongo, 'the whole joint is going sky high!'

'But I'm too groovy to die, baby,' said Shades.

'No time to shoot the breeze, man,' said Thelonious, 'we've gotta split!'

'RUN FOR YOUR LIVES!' screamed the batniks as they beat a hasty retreat. Pandemonium broke out as panic-stricken patrons stampeded out of the building.

Belmont and Burnie were tied fast
to their chairs, unable to move.

'You cut us loose at once!'
demanded Belmont.

'Sorry … no can
do,' said the
Redwitch. 'You've
blown my plans
to smithereens, so
now the Kablooey's
doing the same
to you.'

'And it couldn't happen to a nicer couple of
squares,' added Silas the raven.

With a triumphant screech of laughter the Redwitch
whistled for her broomstick and flew out the door.

Belmont's heart was thumping loudly. He braced himself for the worst as the fuse rapidly burned away to nothing.

THEN SUDDENLY …

... it fizzled.

'Give it to me straight, kid!' cried Burnie with his eyes clamped shut. 'Am I blowed to bits, or what?'

'No, Burnie. It didn't go off,' said Belmont, heaving a sigh of relief.

He managed to wriggle out of his ropes and quickly untied Burnie.

'Let's get this Kablooey back to Professor Cranium. He'll want to find out why it didn't work.'

'No time for that, kid,' said Burnie. 'Somebody's coming! We'd better get outta here … PRONTO!'

Belmont and Burnie climbed out of the window just as the Redwitch stepped cautiously into the room.

'That darn Kablooey must have been a dud,' she mumbled. 'They just don't make things the way they used to.'

She stopped dead in her tracks when she saw her prisoners had fled. '*Nefertiti's nostrils*! They've *escaped*!' she screamed.

Her eyes fell upon the unexploded Kablooey.

'You've got this coming, you pile of useless junk …'

She booted it for all
she was worth.

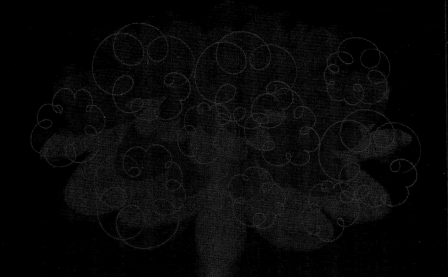

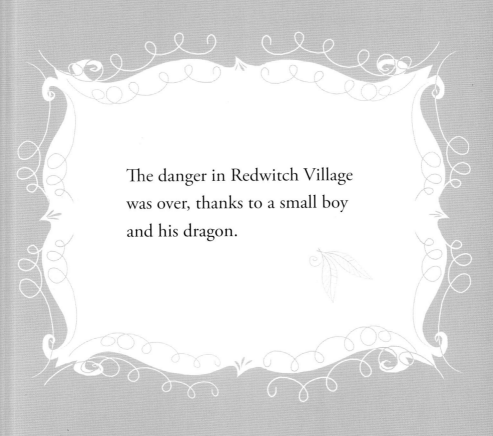

The danger in Redwitch Village was over, thanks to a small boy and his dragon.

Old York Day arrived at last and King Cyrus
unveiled his magnificent gift, the Statue of
Libby, which in time came to represent
Old York's freedom and prosperity to all
the nations of the world.